GIVE UP

DEVMALYA GHOSH

Ddecated to my 1st love

Contents

Preface

Story of a small town boy and his love. struggles with his mind and gives up after losing his way in his life. And Fight with self.

Acknowledgements

Acknowledging to current situation

About The Author

Devmalya Ghosh, 22 years old author was born in Rajarhat kolkata in March 2000. From the age of 16, Devmalya wrote poetries. He's the first poet published in a magazine named Naba parichay Patrika. Recently author working in an MNC and following his passion.

CHAPTER ONE

Give Up

Give up is a strong word, which usually no one likes. but when life will put you in complexes Which word usually came to our mind that is giving up. We can't do anything. After that day when I lost Shefali, I'm becoming like a turtle. Everything is happening beyond my thought process. The plus point and the worst point is she didn't stop talking with me.

I've never felt this bad when people slam me if she'll text me now usually, I've felt that Numb and disappointed

I don't know how bad I've felt. She speaks up every time why you've stolen my arrogance. and as usual, I've lost my words.

After 6 months when we stopped talking to each other suddenly my brother came into my room and says " dada you didn't get the news? " I've replied about which news you are speaking about? Brother says Shefali is married and it's a love marriage.

She escapes from her home to marry that person. Tomorrow is Reception.

I've thanked god and prayed for her happy life, not for mine. after this, I dropped out my college because I'm in a depression phase. Yes, I've given up. We gave up. and it's not raining under the fucking sky. It's raining only from my eyes.

I've lost myself in this mess of love. and today I'm writing I'm thinking of her face her eyes our valuable times. and how we give up.

After her marriage, I started thinking about how life fucked me up. but god never give me rest in terms of thinking. In terms of stress. Baba is not well, he's suffering. That disease caught him which is not recoverable. Cancer, maybe in terms of Zodiac sign is good but not in terms of decease. baba was broken. One day he called me into his room and ask " baba how are you?" I've replied " fine baba how are you? " " first class " I've never thought that this first class will steal my baba. baba left me and left lots of memories with me, lots of regrates and hate for Shefali.

Every day and every night this hate increased only but now we are on the same page of love

Enter Caption

**it is 2nd part of It's Raining under the fucking sky
more to come**

Coming soon